WITCHY'S
Turned Around House

WRITTEN BY MARCIA TRIMBLE   ILLUSTRATED BY CHAD CAMERON

Images Press - Los Altos Hills, California

Publisher's Cataloging-in-Publication
(Provided by Quality Books, Inc.)

Trimble, Marcia
        Witchy's turned around house / by Marcia Trimble;
        illustrated by Chad Cameron.-1st. ed.
        p. cm.
        SUMMARY: Witchy gets into the Witches' Book of Records
        by casting a spell which spins a Nantucket Island summerhouse
        around so that the porch will be protected from the westerlies.
        Preassigned LCCN: 98-93087
        ISBN: 1-891577-27-1
        1. Witches-Juvenile fiction. 2. Nantucket Island
        (Mass.)-Juvenile fiction. 3. Magic-Juvenile fiction.
        1. Cameron, Chad. 11. Title.

PZ7.T734Wi 1998 [E]
QB198-795

10 9 8 7 6 5 4 3 2 1

Set in Mrs. Eaves.
The illustrations are rendered in oil and collage.
BOOK DESIGN: Kevin Fitzgerald and Chad Cameron

Printed in Hong Kong by South China Printing Co. (1988) Ltd. on acid free paper. ∞

E
T 735w

For Malinda,
from whom I learned
the magical power of
children's laughter.
-M.T.

For Momster and Pop
-C.C.

Witchy was in her lab pouring powders and juices into her cauldron…and mixing her brew for the annual spinning contest.

"What can I spin before the stroke of midnight?" Witchy wondered. "Spinning webs or yarns won't win me a listing in the Witches' Book of Records. Any witch can spin webs or yarns."

Witchy peered into the brew! "Ooooooooooh! The Dow's summerhouse out at Wauwinet stands alone between Nantucket Sound and the Atlantic Ocean…perfect for spinning…except for one missing ingredient. It is far from town…far from children's laughter."

Witchy stirred the brew
with all her might and wailed
a spell into her cauldron.
"Let Witchy be clever.
Brew stormy weather
without a sliver of shine…
Brew winds that blow the
spinning sign, spreading
laughter with every gust.

Children's laughter is a must to spin the
house between the ocean and the Sound.
Brew winds that blow laughter from Nantucket
Town to Witchy's cauldron in Wauwinet.
Blow children's laughter in the mix
and whirl it, and swirl it, and spin it.
Hurry! Quick as a mouse. Poof!
Spin the Dow's house!"

Thunder rumbled, lightning flashed,
and rain beat down on the Dow's house.

Lightning streaked across Witchy's
eyes. Her spoon, dripping with the
mixture of powders and juices,
slipped from her fingers and
dropped into the brew. The brew
bubbled up and boiled over.

The bank on the ocean side
of the house pulled away.

The windows broke.
The house filled up
with sand. "FANGLE
DANGLE STOP!"
Witchy blurted out.

Witchy grabbed her broomstick handle and stirred the brew again.
"Make the house new! Make the spell be ever true!" Witchy chanted.

The house slid down the bank toward the sound. Pilings sprung up under the house…and a foundation closed around it. The wind blew the glass into smooth sheets. New shingles covered the house.

"WOWIE WHIZZY WHEW," sighed Witchy…as she flew to the house to sweep out the sand.

Witchy wailed again.
"Send wind that spreads
laughter with every gust.
Children's laughter is a must.
Send wind with children's
laughter in it.
Make the wind blow
from Town to Wauwinet.
Hurry! Quick as
a mouse. Poof!
Spin the Dow's house!"

Puff!…The wind blew a sailboat onto the shore.

Figures jumped out of the boat and paraded by the Dow's house, merrymaking and blowing laughter into the wind.

As the children sailed away, their laughter bounced off the Sound, followed Witchy back to her cauldron, breezed into the brew…and tickled her nose.

"Ooooooooh...kachoo!"
she sneezed...and...

...the house spun around...at the stroke of midnight.

The porch that had faced
the Sound faced the ocean.
The dinner table switched sides, too.

The Keeper of Records granted
Witchy three lucky charms.

...Extra nice is trying twice

...Trying once is nice.

to mix a brew that spins a
house that was never haunted…
to make it loved and wanted
with a porch free from the
westerlies that blow with vigor
and vim when daylight grows
dim and a table for dining with
no beachcombers peering in.

Witchy has the winning spin!

Witchy's name shines in the Witches' Book of Records on nights when the moon is full.

Young witches line up to go on Witchy's midnight tour.

"Welcome! I'm Witchy," she says. "I will be your guide tonight. I will take you for a ride that you will never forget. I will tell you about the brew that...

FREE
BROOM BUGGY
RIDES
to see
TURNED-AROUND HOUSE

FR

'S AUTOGRAPH
Witches Book of
SEE WITCHY'S NAME SHINE

RIDES
BY
MOONLIGHT

MOONLIGHT
NIGHTS
ONLY

ooooooooooh…turned a
house…kachoo…around!" she sneezes…
and revs up her broom buggy…